DOG IN DANGER

The story of Sidney and the
Hedgehogs

Hiawyn Oram

Illustrated by
Judith Lawton

ORCHARD BOOKS

Read about your favourite animals in
these other Animal Heroes...

Dolphin SOS!
The story of Nemo and Lemo

Monkey in Space
The story of Chi

Cat in a Corner
The story of Robertson

Sidney's owner
was going on holiday.
He didn't know
what to do with Sidney.
So he put him in his car
and drove.

He drove sixty miles
and then left him
on a strange street
in a strange town
in the pouring rain.
Sidney had never felt so
frightened in his life.
He huddled in a doorway.

"What's happening…"
he whimpered.
"Please someone
tell me what's going on?"
"Well, if you ask me…"
a dripping-wet Setter
was sniffing him all over,
"you've been abandoned."

Sidney's wet hair stood on end.
"ABANDONED?"
"Yes," said the Setter.
"Taken from your nice warm home
and DUMPED.
What did you do?
Mess on the carpet
once too often?"
Before Sidney could answer
the Setter's owner appeared.
"Blessed! Here my beauty!"

The Setter bounded off.
"Keep on the move!"
she barked back.
"That's my advice.
Trust nothing.
Let no one near!"
Sidney put his tail
between his legs
and set off.
Past warehouses.

Between cars.
Up the quay.

Down the quay.
Up and down the backstreets.

At night
he curled up
on dark doorsteps.
But he didn't sleep.
He kept his eyes open
and his ears pricked.

He tried not to think about
his hunger pains.
Then one morning
while slinking down
an alley he noticed
some dustbins.

"Grease and old gravy,"
he sniffed.
"It will have to do."
He stood on his hind legs
and knocked off a lid.
It rolled down the cobblestones.

A woman opened a window.
"Get out of there!"
she yelled.
A man appeared
waving a stick.
"Go on! Get out of it! Scavenger!"

Sidney cowered against
the wall and slopped past.
The man's stick
whizzed past him.
It missed –
but Sidney was terrified.

He tore down the alley
into the road.
He didn't look.
He didn't think.
There was a screech of brakes.
Sidney heard himself yelp.

Every part of him hurt.
People were gathering round.
Trust nothing. Let no one near...
he remembered.
Making a huge effort
he picked himself up
and ran for it.
Then everything went dark.

"Mongrel. Dog. About 5 years."
A vet at the RSPCA
was examining him.
"General condition good.
Hit by car.
No broken bones.
Badly shocked
and very frightened."

Sidney quivered
as the vet's hands moved
over him.
He could see Blessed the Setter
and her owner
in the waiting room.
What were they doing here?
What, for that matter,
was he doing here?

Blessed got up
to explain.
"Ran straight into
a car, didn't you?"
she barked.
"Lucky we were in
the one behind.
Saw everything.
Brought you in."
Blessed's owner told her to
hush and got out her lead.
"Well, got to go now.
Going on a mega-walk.
On the moors, don't you know.
Wish you could come
but he says
you're in good hands here."

"When will I see you again?"
Sidney tried to bark back.
But all he could manage
was a pitiful whimper.

"There, there,"
the vet handed him to
Matty the nurse.
"You'll be all right with us…"
"You certainly will,"
said Matty.

"Now what's your name?"
"Sidney," whimpered Sidney.
Matty fiddled with his collar.
"Sidney," she read.
"That's what I said," said Sidney.
"All right, Sidney," said Matty
carrying him into her office.
"D'you know what
I'm going to do?
I'm going to keep you
here with me
until you're feeling better."
"If I ever do," sniffed Sidney.

But within a few days
- to Sidney's surprise -
he did feel better.
"Almost like my old self again!
And since you've looked
after me so well I'm going
to do a few things for you."
Then Sidney set about
making himself useful.
He kept the cats in order.
He comforted
stray dogs.

He appointed
himself official
Night Watchdog
and Nurse Matty's
personal bodyguard.

"Oh Sidney!"
she cried one morning.
"How we're going to
miss you when you're gone."
"Miss me? When I'm gone?"
Sidney was shocked.
This was his home now.
Wasn't it?
He wasn't going anywhere.
Was he?

Nurse Matty, he decided,
must be mistaken.
He jumped up and licked her tears.
"Don't cry," he comforted her.
"I won't leave you."
"Oh dear, dear Sidney,"
Nurse Matty picked him up.
"You don't understand, do you?
Dogs can't stay here for ever.
If no one claims them
they go to our re-homing kennels.
And if there's no room there
then we have to..."

A cold chill shot through Sidney.
"Nonsense!" he barked.
"I won't hear anymore.
And that's all there is to it.
Now even if you haven't,
I have work to do!"

For the rest of the morning
Sidney kept himself very busy
so he didn't have to think
about Matty's words.
He alerted the staff
to a sick gerbil.

He rescued a puppy
from under the fridge.

Then he went to
check out a cardboard box
that had appeared by
the radiator in
Nurse Matty's office.

He sniffed carefully round it.
He peered carefully over the top.
"Oh my goodness!"
He nearly jumped out of his skin.

In the box
were four hedgehogs.
Four very newborn hedgehogs.
So newborn their eyes
hadn't even opened.
"You poor little mites!"
Sidney was most upset.

"Lost your mother
to a car, I expect!
Well, your mother
I am not but next best
will have to do!"
Then very carefully
so as not to crush them
he climbed into the box
and lay down.
And immediately the
little hedgehogs stirred and
squeaked softly.
Then one by one
they wriggled towards
Sidney's warmth.

"It's astonishing!" Nurse Matty and
the staff stared down.
"He's adopted them!"
Sidney looked up proudly.
"Well of course!
Four babes in need.
Wouldn't you?
Anyway, you're off the hook.
I'm in charge here."

And in charge
was what Sidney was.
He kept the tiny creatures
warm and clean.
He gave them each a name
so he could call out to them
when he wasn't in their box.

He helped them to eat
and drink and guarded them
like a tigress
guarding her young.
And in his care they
began to thrive.
They opened their eyes.
Their soft spines began
to harden and they took
their first wobbly steps.

Nurse Matty and the staff
were very proud of him.
"Sidney!" they said.
"Do you know we believe
that without you
those little things
might have died."
"Criminal!" barked Sidney.

"Yes!" said Nurse Matty,
with a funny look in her eye.
"And surely one rescue
deserves another."
She strode into
her office and picked up
the telephone excitedly.

A short time later
four photographers and three
newspaper reporters arrived.
They wanted Sidney's
photograph – with his charges,
of course!
Flash! Flash! Flash!

They also wanted
Sidney's story.
Nurse Matty gave
it to them as far as
she knew it with
only a few corrections
from Sidney.

And a few days later
Matty told Sidney
the great news.
"You're a star, Sidney.
You're in all the papers.
And best of all
the telephone hasn't
stopped ringing!"
"So what!" barked Sidney.
He was watching
his adopted children playing.

And he was worried.
They were growing up
and growing prickly.

So Matty explained.
People were ringing up
because they'd read
about Sidney adopting
the orphaned hedgehogs.
"And now they all want
 to ADOPT YOU!"

"Well, I never!"
Sidney blushed.
"But don't worry,"
said Matty,
"this time only the
very best will do."

And while Sidney
got used to the
idea of his children
growing up and
having their own
lives, Nurse Matty
began meeting
possible new
owners for Sidney.

She was very strict.
She asked lots and lots
of questions about how
they'd look after him.
And that was how
a week later
Sidney found himself
at home
with The Bests.

There was Mr and Mrs Best,
Ben, Susie, Rachel
and Fred Best.

There was Nigel the hamster

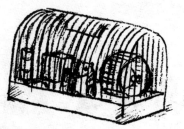

Tigger the cat

Sarah the Jack Russell

and a cage full of stick insects.

There was also
Blessed the Setter
right next door.

All of them –
except the stick insects perhaps –
soon adored Sidney.
"What a bit of brilliant luck!"
said Blessed
as they talked
over the fence.
"After all your troubles
to be adopted

by my good neighbours
the Bests!"
"It certainly is," sighed Sidney.
"And do you know the best part?
Even better than the long walks
and the real bones
and the grooming
and the cuddles?"

"No," said Blessed, "tell me."
"I don't even feel adopted,"
said Sidney.
"I feel I've always
been one of the Bests."

DOG IN DANGER
is based on a true story
of a mongrel called Sidney
who was found abandoned
in the town of Baltry
in South Yorkshire
some years ago.
The author has changed
the names of all the people
and put words into
the animals' mouths.

Here are some other Orchard books about animals that you might enjoy...

PIPE DOWN, PRUDLE!
1 85213 766 5 (hbk) 1 85213 770 3 (pbk)

RHODE ISLAND ROY
1 85213 764 9 (hbk) 1 85213 768 1 (pbk)

WELCOME HOME, BARNEY
1 85213 765 7 (hbk) 1 85213 769 X (pbk)

WE WANT WILLIAM!
1 85213 763 0 (hbk) 1 85213 767 3 (pbk)

A FORTUNE FOR YO-YO
1 85213 583 2 (hbk) 1 85213 679 0 (pbk)

SLEEPY SAMMY
1 85213 584 0 (hbk) 1 85213 677 4 (pbk)